Sharks

Dogfish

Hammerhead

Great White

# Fish School

## Nancy Poydar

Holiday House / New York

Text and illustrations copyright © 2009 by Nancy Poydar
All Rights Reserved
HOLIDAY HOUSE is registered in the U.S. Patent and Trademark Office.
Printed and Bound in Malaysia
The text typeface is Hank. The art for this book was created in gouache.
www.holidayhouse.com
First Edition
1 3 5 7 9 10 8 6 4 2
Library of Congress Cataloging-in-Publication Data
Poydar, Nancy.
Fish school / Nancy Poydar. – 1st ed.
p. cm.
Summary: Charlie tries to educate his pet goldfish by taking him to school and to the aquarium on a class trip.
Includes tips on the care and feeding of goldfish.
ISBN 978-0-8234-2140-4 (hardcover)
[1. Goldfish – Fiction. 2. Pets – Fiction. 3. Aquariums, Public – Fiction. 4. School field trips – Fiction.] I. Title.
PZ7.P8846Fk 2009   [E] – dc22   2008022576

## A guide to the fish in this book:

p. 2: clockwise, from top left: Fantail Goldfish, Common Goldfish, Calico Goldfish, Angelfish / pp. 5, 6, 9, 28, 31: Fantail Goldfish / p. 12: Sea Jellies / p. 13, clockwise, from top left: Giant Gourami, Tinfoil Barbs, Giant Gourami, Common Carp, Freshwater Turtle, Common Carp / pp. 14-15, clockwise, from top left: Sharks, Squirrelfish, Marble Grouper, Yellowmouthed Groupers, Eel, Barracuda, Misty Groupers, Blue Chromis, Sea Turtle, Angelfish, Silvery Lookdown Fish, Blue-Striped Grunt, Ray, Blue Chromis, Blue-Striped Grunt / pp. 16-17, 27, 29: Dolphins / pp. 18-19: Whale Shark (hanging).

In large tank (clockwise, from top left): Sharks, Squirrelfish, Dogfish, (bottom left) Blue Chromis, Barracuda, Sea Turtle, Eel, Ray. / p. 19: In left tank: Striped Bass. In right tank: Trout. / p. 20, left to right: Tinfoil Barbs, Giant Gourami, Tiger Barbs, Puffers / pp. 21, 22-23: Moon Jellies / p. 24: Left tank: Giant Gourami (top), Tinfoil Barbs (bottom). Top tank: Moon Jellies / p. 25: Sharks

This book is for Brooke

Special thanks to
Bill Simpkins
Director of Education
The National Aquarium
Washington, D.C.
and his staff

and

Kathy Devaney
Newtonville Pet
Newtonville, MA

Charlie got a goldfish for his birthday. He loved it more than any other present. "I'm going to teach you everything I learn!" he told Wishy.

*Swish, swish* went Wishy in his bowl.

Charlie brought Wishy to school for Show-and-Tell.

"Fish are my specialty," Charlie told the class. "I'm teaching Wishy like people teach dolphins. I'm getting a tank for him."

"Goldfish are freshwater fish," said Ms. Finn. "They don't swim in the ocean with dolphins. And dolphins aren't fish; they're mammals! But some people say you can train goldfish."

Then Ms. Finn asked, "Who would like to go to the aquarium?" Everyone wanted to go, especially Charlie.

The night before the aquarium trip, Charlie said, "Wishy, I'm going to teach you everything I learn at the aquarium."

*Swish, swish* went Wishy's tail.

Then an idea bubbled up in Charlie's head. Why not, he thought.

On the way to the aquarium, Charlie imagined the bus was a school of fish. It swam past cars and beside trucks.

"We're a school of fish," Charlie whispered to his backpack.

"Pick a favorite part of the trip," said Ms. Finn. "We'll make picture-stories back at school."

Inside the aquarium, Charlie said, "Look! The fish are dancing."

"The sea jellies aren't fish," said Ms. Finn. "They don't have any bones or gills."

"The sea jellies aren't fish," whispered Charlie.

"Over here," Ms. Finn said, "are freshwater fish, like your Wishy, Charlie."

"Maybe this will be the favorite part," whispered Charlie.

"Everyone picks his or her own favorite!" said Libby.

Around the corner, a tank of seawater reached up
through the ceiling. "Here are the sharks, barracudas, and
eels," Charlie said to his backpack. "You make a better pet!"

"I'm not a pet," said Simone.

"Look, some fish are in schools!" said Charlie.

Ms. Finn said, "Fish swim in schools so they won't get gobbled up!"

Finally they reached the dolphin arena. "This will be our favorite part," said Charlie.
"You're talking to your backpack!" said Simone.
"What backpack?" said Charlie.

Just then a dolphin
jumped up and touched
a ball.
"Wow!" said Charlie.
"Cool!" said Simone.

When it was time to get back on the bus, no one wanted to leave.

"Can't we stay longer?" pleaded Simone.

But they had to follow Ms. Finn, swooping together like a school of fish, back around the giant ocean tank, through the freshwater gallery, and to the jellies.

"The dolphins were the best part," whispered Charlie. "Now who are you talking to?" asked Simone. "You're not wearing your backpack."

"Yikes! Wishy's in my backpack!" cried Charlie.

"You brought Wishy?" Ms. Finn was astonished.
"I want him to learn what I learn," sputtered Charlie.
"Now we CAN'T leave," insisted Simone. "Wishy could
be gobbled up . . . by **sharks**!"

Everyone cried, "Find Wishy!"

"We'll stay together," said Ms. Finn.

"Like a school of fish!" said Charlie.

"Wishy's not by the jellies," yelled Simone.

"Wishy's not by the freshwater tanks!" hollered Libby.

"Wishy's not by the giant ocean tank!" called Thomas.

In the dolphin arena, no one could see a backpack.
"Charlie," said Simone, "I remember. You put it under a seat!"
Everyone dived under the seats.

"My backpack!" hollered Charlie, coming up for air and holding Wishy. *Swish, swish* went Wishy in his Ziploc bag. Everyone shouted and clapped.

"Wishy, you're a star!" whispered Charlie.

"Wishy, you're lucky to be alive!" said Ms. Finn.

The next day, Ms. Finn said it was time to
make aquarium picture-stories.
"I know what part was the best," said Libby.
"Me too!" shouted Thomas.
"So do I," said Simone.

"Wishy, all the aquarium picture-stories are about you!" whispered Charlie.
*Swish, swish* went Wishy, *SWISH, SWISH.*

# Charlie's Fish School
## by Charlie

Goldfish are not as smart as dolphins, but they can learn to do things for food, such as come to the top of the water when you are about to feed them.

Lots of goldfish aren't GOLD. In fact, goldfish can change colors during their lifetime.

A little goldfish can grow up to eight or twelve inches.

A goldfish usually lives to be twelve years old, but some live to be twenty. A goldfish named Tish lived to be forty-three years old!

One goldfish needs a tank with at least ten gallons of water in it to swim in. The tank should also have a filter and plants.

If a goldfish hasn't finished its meal in five minutes, it has been fed too much fish food.

Goldfish have no eyelids! Keep them out of the sun.

Even though your goldfish is a pet, you shouldn't pet it. Petting a fish could hurt its scales.

It is tricky to transport a goldfish. WISHY IS LUCKY TO BE ALIVE after his trip to the aquarium in a plastic bag!